Unk's Fiddle

Unk's Fiddle

STORIES TO TOUCH THE HEART

STEVE BURT
Storyteller of the Heart

Burt Creations

Unk's Fiddle

First Hardcover Printing 1995
ISBN 0-9649283-0-2

First Paperback Printing 2001
ISBN: 0-9649283-6-1
Printed in USA

Inquiries should be addressed to:

Burt Creations

Steve Burt
29 Arnold Place
Norwich, CT 06360

T 866-693-6936
F 860-889-4068
www.burtcreations.com

SINGING PRAISES ♪

*"**Unk's Fiddle** is one of those beautiful tragedies that we love to cry over and which also reveals a bit of human nature. Steve Burt's touching but not maudlin story leaves us satisfied but thinking . . . Unk had a full life, but couldn't there have been-more? In my opinion, a story that leaves us thinking is the best kind."*
— Liz Aleshire, Fiction Editor,
New England Writers' Network

"Steve Burt's stories have a wonderful way of engaging readers with their human touch. He is a gifted storyteller."
— Linda Davidson, Editor, *Church Worship Magazine*

"A heartwarming collection from an author with a flair for writing about small town characters and situations with authority and accuracy. Truly 'Chicken Soup for the Soul,' and with a warm grilled cheese sandwich to boot!"
— Kris Ferrazza, Maine Journalist of the Year

"With a few deft brushstrokes Steve Burt paints backdrops that add life and color to these heart-touching stories. His richly textured tales draw you in the way a great painting does, turning observers into participants."
— Watercolorist Mary Staggs, St. Petersburg, FL

Thanks to

. . . all the small press editors who printed my stories and built my confidence.

. . . Dotti Albertine at Albertine Graphic Design in Santa Monica, who designed the front and back covers and the book's interior.

. . . Ellen Reid of Smarketing in Los Angeles, who has been the ramrod (organizer / team coordinator / you name it) for several of my projects now. She, more than anyone, saw my potential as a popular author.

. . . My wife, Jo Ann, whose daytime jobs helped finance both the hardcover and paperback printings.

About the Author

STEVE BURT'S life reads like one of his stories; it's a good life, a genuine life, with plenty of plot to make it interesting.

Since 1979 Steve has been a pastor, church consultant, seminary professor, church executive, and very popular keynote speaker, mixing humor and stories in with his teaching.

Graduating high school complete with academic and sports honors and having edited the school newspaper, Steve went into the Navy for a four-year hitch. He wrote for the ship newsletter, continued to excel at sports, and in 1969 married his high school sweetheart, Jo Ann. The next year their daughter, Wendy, was born.

In 1983 Steve received a Masters Degree from Bangor Theological Seminary. In 1987 he completed a four-year doctorate program in three years and graduated at the top of his class at Andover Newton Theological School.

In addition to stories that touch the heart, like those in *Unk's Fiddle*, Steve also writes stories that chill the heart, *Odd Lot,* and warm the heart, *A Christmas Dozen.*

Not what you might expect from your average Reverend Doctor / Pastor / Author. But somehow it's right on target for Steve Burt. What's next? Stay tuned.

Also by Steve Burt

North & South Fork Car-Top Canoeist's Guide to Eastern Long Island Creeks and Waterways
with Austin C. Burt
Canu-U?! Rentals 1976

Activating Leadership in the Small Church
Clergy and Laity Working Together
Judson Press 1988

Fingerprints on the Chalice
Contemporary Communion Meditations
CSS Publishing 1990

Christmas Special Delivery
Stories and Meditations for Christmas
Fairway Press 1991

Raising Small Church Esteem
with Hazel R. Roper
Alban Institute 1992

My Lord, He's Loose in the World!
Meditations on the Meaning of Easter
Brentwood Christian Press 1994

What Do You Say to a Burning Bush?
Sermons for the Season After Pentecost
CSS Publishing 1995

Unk's Fiddle (Hardcover)
Steven E. Burt 1995

The Little Church That Could
Raising Small Church Esteem
(re-release of 1992 book)
Judson Press 2000

A Christmas Dozen
Christmas Stories to Warm the Heart
Steven E. Burt 2000

Odd Lot
Stories to Chill the Heart
Paperback October 2001

Short Story Acknowledgments

"Unk's Fiddle" first in *Peconic Bay Shopper*, April 1994, later in *Green Mountain Trading Post, Five Stones, New England Writers' Network, Lines in the Sand, Northern Reader, Show & Tell, Tucumcari Literary Review, New Press Literary Quarterly, Who's Who in the Short-Shorts Digest, Vermont Voices III, Healing Inn, Coastal Journal, Reader's Break, Northern New England Review, Hometown Journal.* It also received *Storyteller Magazine's* Reader's Choice Award (Jan-Feb-Mar 1999), *My Legacy Magazine's* Editor's Choice Award (Nov 2000), and was selected for *Chicken Soup for the Single's Soul.*

"Christmas 1944" first in *Peconic Bay Shopper*, December 1986, later in *Valley News, Compassion: Literary Quarterly for Social Responsibility, Green Mountain Trading Post, Ebbing Tide New England Writers' Network, Suffolk Times Holiday Supplement, Northern New England Review, Church Worship, Vermont Ink, Hometown News.* Also in author's *A Christmas Dozen: Christmas Stories to Warm the Heart,* 2000.

"Neighbors" first in *Oxalis 23*, 1994, later in *New England Writers' Network, Who's Who in the Short-Shorts, Peconic Bay Shopper, The Crunge, Glory Hole Review, Portable Wall, Vermont Voices III,* and *Storyteller*.

"Peevil's Eyebrow" first in *Lines in the* Sand, September 1994, later in *Peconic Bay Shopper, Show & Tell, Reader's Break: A Literary Anthology, Magnolia Leaf, Northern Reader,* and *Storyteller*.

"The Ice Fisherman" first in *Peconic Bay Shopper*, September 1994, later in *Green Mountain Trading Post, Belletrist Review, Potpourri, Potomac Review, Reader's Break,* and *Vermont Voices III.*

"The Trellis" first in *Peconic Bay* Shopper, August 1978 after it won First Place in the Southold Town (NY) short story contest, later in *Green Mountain Trading Post, Green Mountain Gazette,* and *Who's Who in the Short-Shorts Digest.* Copyright 1978 by Steve Burt. All rights reserved.

"The Magi's Gift" first in *Dogwood Tales,* November 1994, later in *Ebbing Tide* (prize-winner), *Peconic Bay Shopper, Lincoln County Weekly, The Suffolk Times, Show & Tell, My Legacy, Vermont Ink,* and *Church Worship.* Also in author's *A Christmas Dozen: Christmas Stories to Warm the Heart,* 2000. Copyright 1993 by Steve Burt. All rights reserved.

"Perfect, Just Perfect" (a.k.a. "Just Like I Knew") first in *Peconic Bay Shopper,* December 1978, reprinted more times than anyone can keep up with, both with and without permission. Also in author's *A Christmas Dozen: Christmas Stories to Warm the Heart,* 2000. Copyright 1975 by Steve Burt. All rights reserved.

"Garden By the River" first in *Green Mountain Trading Post,* July 1992 (as "Witchy Woman's Garden"), later in *Peconic Bay Shopper.* The "frame" was later dropped and the interior horror story became "Garden Plot," which appeared in *Vermont Ink, Frightmares, Goddess of the Bay, New Dawn Fades, My Legacy* (Editor's Choice Award), *Beyond the Moon* (Second Place, Horror), *All Hallows* (England's Ghost Story Society). Honorable Mention in *Year's Best Fantasy & Horror.* Also in author's *Odd Lot: Stories to Chill the Heart.* Copyright 1991 by Steve Burt. All rights reserved.

"Woo Woo" first in *Peconic Bay Shopper,* August 1994, later in *New Press Literary Quarterly* and *Ebbing Tide* (First Prize, Fiction). Copyright 1994 by Steve Burt. All rights reserved.

"The Thumb Island Elephants" first in *Peconic Bay Shopper,* December 1995 and *Green Mountain Trading Post,* December 1995, later in *Church Worship.* Also in author's *A Christmas Dozen: Christmas Stories to Warm the* Heart, 2000. Copyright 1994 by Steve Burt. All rights reserved.

"Whinny" first in *Peconic Bay Shopper,* May 1994, later in *Dogwood Tales, Ultimate Writer, Storyteller,* and *Vermont Ink.* Copyright 1994 by Steve Burt. All rights reserved.

INTRODUCTION

Each and every one of these award winning short stories delivers two things right from the start, and delivers them consistently from the first page to the last. They are: **wonderful characters and captivating stories**.

Steve Burt's people come alive the instant we meet them. It is more like they are old friends, not new folks whose acquaintance we are just making. How, after reading just a few lines, we can feel like we have known these people forever is one of those mysteries of great writing. Steve Burt knows the secret.

As for great stories, storytelling is an art all its own. These stories start with a bang that grabs your attention and end as you sigh at the last line. They have a beginning, a middle and an end—that you don't really want to reach because you want to spend more time with these people.

Part of the secret is that Steve has the rare ability to observe, then recount the essence of what he's seen. That makes his stories genuine. Sure, they may come from his imagination—and a vivid imagination it is—but at their heart, they are real.

Unk's Fiddle is a book to have on your bookshelf, or by your bedside. And it's a book to make sure your friends and loved ones have in their libraries as well, even if you have to buy it for them yourself.

Like you, they will become hooked after the first couple of lines. Do you doubt it? Go ahead, open to any story and read the first paragraph. Bet you can't stop.

CONTENTS

Unk's Fiddle

Unk played the violin—well, he called it a fiddle—but he'd never play it when anyone was around. Except for Eleanor. He'd play it for her. But then they'd been friends for over seventy years, since they were babies.

I think Unk was always sweet on her. That's not to say they dated or anything, not like going to the movies or out to dinner—Mom said they never did that.

"Just passionate friends," Mom would say, and try as I might to read into what she'd said, I never heard her snicker nor caught a wink when she said it. Nor did she even hint that there might be anything sexual in her use of the word passionate.

Neither of them ever married. Eleanor was referred to as Perryville's old maid, but never with any maliciousness to the phrase. And Unk, everybody jokingly called him Perryville's most eligible bachelor, which was kind of ironic because Unk wasn't much to look at. He was short, with liver spots on his forehead that continued on up over his bald dome. His right eye was dried up from a metal shaving that flew into it when he was a teenager running a grinding wheel at the mill. His face was pock-marked from some awful acne that had plagued him in his younger years. And his knee had been crushed when a stack of logs broke loose off a railroad flatcar he and a friend were unloading with horses. Both of the horses and his friend were crushed to death, and Unk said he'd always considered himself fortunate to escape with only a draggy limp.

Eleanor was the only child of a couple who had run the dry goods store in town. She ran it alone for awhile after her parents died, but sold it to a man from Brattleboro when it got to be too much. She taught Sunday school at the Congregational Church–children for many years, then an adult Bible class after she turned fifty. That's when Unk, who had dropped out of church when he was ten, had started attending her adult class and became a regular member. Eleanor also sang in the choir–she had a lovely alto voice and occasionally sang solos–and served at church suppers and sewed for the Ladies Aid. It was rumored that she played the harmonica, but not in public. The church seemed to be the extent of her social life, except for having Unk come by Saturday nights with his fiddle.

Unk was Grampa's brother and had lived with Grampa and Grandma most of his life, working the farm. When they died and left him the place, he surprised everyone by selling it and moving in with us.

We fixed up a room for him in the loft over the garage. Since the garage had been built onto the back of our house, it meant Unk's room shared a common wall with my bedroom. The wall was thicker than an interior wall, of course, because it had once been the clapboarded back wall of the house. Yet despite its thickness, once I was in bed I could hear Unk playing that fiddle–every night except Saturday when he was at Eleanor's. The music was faint and I couldn't make out all the notes, but on a good night it would work its way through the wall sweet and mournful, never the scratchy sound I expected a violin to make (an expectation I developed from watching Alfalfa in the Our Gang comedies).

When he wasn't using them, Unk's fiddle and bow hung on the wall above his bed. I never saw them there, because I was never in his room. I figured it out in later years when he got the tremors. After he finished playing for the night, I'd hear the fiddle k-k-klunking against our common wall as his hand shook while he tried to put it back in place.

When I was eleven or twelve, Unk and I went fishing at Thatcher Pond. As I fumbled to get a worm on my hook, Unk mumbled, "Eleanor baits a hook faster'n that."

At first I thought he was jibing me, but then I recalled the tone and the way he'd said it, and I turned the sentence over in my head. He hadn't said it to put me down–that wasn't in his voice. In fact, he wasn't talking to me at all, not really. He was talking to himself, out loud, simply stating an observation, maybe a fact: Eleanor Fawcett, the old maid who played a harmonica when nobody was around, a woman nobody ever saw fish (at least not to my knowledge), could bait a hook pretty darned fast. Unk knew.

Later, as we were packing up to leave, Unk put his arm around my shoulder and told me how much he loved to fish. He said selling the farm was the best thing he'd ever done, because it gave him time to do the things he loved. He didn't tell me what it was he loved, but if he could have mouthed the words, I expect they'd have ushered forth in a holy whisper: fishing, fiddling, and Eleanor. I tried to imagine Unk and Eleanor after Saturday dinner, sitting in her parlor, tapping their toes and conversing through their fiddle and harmonica.

One afternoon I was on my hands and knees in the garden, pulling carrots and handing them to Unk. I asked him why he only played the fiddle in private. He looked at me as if debating whether to tell, then said, "When I was ten, I was learning my dad's fiddle. Dad played barn dances. One day I mentioned to Reverend Hotchkiss, who's dead now, that I hoped to be good enough to play in church some day. He shook his head no, and told me a fiddle ain't suitable for church music and giving glory to God."

Unk was silent for a moment, and when I looked up at him, his face was set like granite. I guessed that was the year Unk stopped going to church.

Unk was seventy-nine when Eleanor died. She was seventy-eight. She simply didn't wake up one Tuesday morning, just as Unk, ten years later, would fail to wake up one Tuesday morning.

Her viewing hours were Friday night. Mom, Dad, and I went. Unk refused. He stayed in his room, saying he preferred to remember her the way he'd last seen her. I thought she looked fine, in a pretty black dress with pink and purple flowers on it. Her hands were folded on her stomach as if praying, which seemed to me appropriate, and her knuckles didn't look gnarly or arthritic. I tried to imagine those fingers baiting a hook.

Next day the church was full for the funeral. Unk didn't go with us when we left the house in the car. He said he'd catch up, but I doubted he'd show, not without the car to get there. And after all, he hadn't been able to face the visiting hours.

As the pews filled up, Mrs. King played a medley of

old hymns on the organ. Eleanor's two elderly cousins from New Hampshire, her only blood family, sat in the front pew. The choir sang *In the Garden* and *Abide with Me,* two of Eleanor's favorites.

Reverend Winters read a handful of scripture passages, including one about running the race with perseverance and fighting the good fight, which made me wonder if Eleanor had been in some lifelong struggle I hadn't been aware of. He offered a brief eulogy, then asked if anyone cared to share any memories about Eleanor or to offer any words of thanksgiving for her life.

Roberta Gerrity spoke for the choir, saying "Eleanor was a faithful and committed choir member who inspired us all." A man stood and spoke of being inspired by the Sunday school teacher Eleanor. He sat down and there followed a long, uncomfortable silence. No one else spoke. I wanted to fill the void myself, but I didn't know what to say and my body felt heavy as a stone.

That's when Unk limped down the aisle, fiddle in his left hand, bow in his right. He was dripping sweat from the mile walk in from the house. He walked slowly, shyly, reverently. His head was bent and he trudged, trudged like a man climbing a gallows. When he reached the golden oak communion table with the carved *In Remembrance of Me* across its front, he looked out over the congregation. He wanted to speak, but his lips only trembled. Tears mixed with the streams of sweat on his face. The saltiness must have stung his eyes, because he blinked and blinked. I wanted to run up and comfort him, but I couldn't move.

Unk raised the fiddle to his shoulder, cradled it

under his chin, and drew the bow across the strings. He began with *Amazing Grace,* slipped seamlessly into *Greensleeves*, then wove together strains from both into a sound more mournful and sweeter than any I've ever heard. We cried then, the whole church and I, to watch and hear Unk honor and weep for Eleanor through his fiddle. When he stopped, we sat stunned. Unk walked out, fiddle and bow in hand, and trudged home.

No music seeped through my wall for months after that.

Then one morning Unk came down to breakfast, smiled, and said, "Want to fish Thatcher's?"

By mid-morning we had a beautiful brown trout.

That night I lay in bed, thinking about the trout, the warm sun, and how good it felt to have Unk back. Then I heard it–Unk's fiddle singing.

I think he played in his room every night after that until his dying day. And many a night, I swear I don't know how, Unk made that fiddle wail and cry, just like a harmonica.

Christmas 1944

The soldier's hollow eyes scanned the farmyard in the dusk. A broken chimney bowed like a mourner over the smoking ruins. Before the artillery shelling a tidy white farmhouse had graced the countryside. Now there was only a mix of rubble and charred timbers.

"Helluva Christmas Eve. Not even sure if I'm in Belgium, France, or Luxembourg," the soldier mumbled. "Can't very well send Christmas cards if I don't know the return address. Maybe I'm on the corner."

A splintered pony cart caught his eye. One of the shells had exploded nearby and overturned it. "Somehow, I'd have imagined it more scenic."

The barn was still standing. Perhaps because there had been little wind and perhaps because the house and barn were 100 yards apart, no spark had jumped. On the path from the house to the barn lay a hound, its chest blown open, innards spilling out. A dead chicken lay nearby. Nothing moved.

"Just another casualty," the soldier muttered with bitterness, "in a long list of casualties." He picked up the chicken by its feet, held it at arm's length, and tossed it aside. "Not even a Christmas goose this year."

Something moved. Barn door. He dropped to the ground with his finger on the trigger and waited for an enemy soldier to step out. His breath stopped and his heart pounded fast and hard.

A kitten. A white kitten. As it pushed past the door, the hollow-eyed soldier felt his muscles relax and his breath rush out. "No," he whispered. "There still might be someone inside." His finger tightened on the trigger again as he decided what to do.

It was dusk. He had been separated from his outfit. It was Christmas Eve in a war zone, he was bone-tired, and he wasn't even sure what country he was in. He needed a place to sleep, and it was either the barn or the woods. But he wasn't sure the barn was empty.

Nothing moved for five minutes, so he changed his position, working around to the back of the barn. He didn't trust the front. Too risky. Behind the barn he discovered a fenced stock pen with a low door leading inside. He entered cautiously, rifle barrel first.

The barn was dark and empty. The animals had either escaped, been eaten, or, like the hound and the chicken, been killed in the shelling. The stalls were empty except for the loose straw scattered for bedding. There was no hay. The Allied advance had turned the hayfields into battlefields.

The soldier looked into the rafters. There were two identical lofts, one on each end of the barn.

"Helluva Christmas Eve," he said, and climbed the ladder to one of the lofts. Once up, he moved to a corner and pulled off his pack.

"Where's Santa with my presents tonight?" he mumbled sarcastically. "I guess he and God stay clear of the war zone."

The soldier sat dazed for a moment, stunned by the possibility of what he had uttered. Finally he took off his helmet, set it aside, and began pulling things from his pack.

A can of beans. Powdered milk. Two chocolate bars. The beautiful knitted shawl he had bought in a French village. He hoped to send it home to his mother, but in truth he simply prayed he might get home alive to give it to her himself. He opened the beans and ate them along with one of the chocolate bars. Then he lay on the loose straw and fell asleep.

A noise woke him, and he sat bolt upright, rifle ready. No idea how long he'd slept. Not sure if it was night or day. A dim light. Was it dawn? It was lantern light. He inched to the edge of the loft and peered down.

A young woman, hardly more than a child herself, sat on a bed of straw, nursing a baby. The child cooed as it sucked, and the mother sang a lullaby. No father or traveling companion to be seen. The hollow-eyed soldier kept silent.

After a while the young mother lay back on the straw and lifted the child above her head. The baby gurgled and giggled each time she lowered it to her face and kissed its belly. Once she held it overhead and it drooled on her, but she simply laughed and kept on. She sat up and kissed its bottom, then lay the baby across her lap and stroked its back and hair. The child flailed its arms and legs but didn't fall asleep. When it tried to turn over and look up, the young mother stood up, putting one hand behind the baby's head and another under its bottom. Then the two of them began to dance, swirling and dipping around the dirt floor together. The mother's long skirt kicked up tiny straw and dust whirlwinds, and the white kitten swiped at her with its paw.

The breathless young mother slowed to a waltz until the baby fell asleep. Then she walked to a horse stall, spread a white linen napkin on the straw, and laid the sleeping baby on it. She covered it with a second linen napkin, bowed her head, and silently prayed.

Another movement. From the other loft. The soldier's hollow eyes met another pair of hollow eyes. The enemy. Each had been intent on the mother and child. Now they were intent on each other. For a long time neither moved. Neither raised a weapon. Then, as if by design, both turned to the mother bowed over her sleeping child.

The enemy moved first, and the hollow-eyed soldier watched as his counterpart cautiously slung the rifle over his shoulder and began the climb down from the loft.

The sound of boots on the ladder startled the mother, and she looked up afraid. But when the soldier smiled and nodded respectfully, she relaxed a little and acknowledged his nod.

He knelt, reached a hand into his pack, and drew out a carved wooden box. When he lifted its lid, a waltz began. The mother smiled as he held out the music box to her. Not a word was spoken. After a moment of silence, the enemy soldier stood, slipped on his pack, and disappeared into the night.

In the loft, the hollow-eyed soldier waited to see if his enemy would return, but when nothing happened after ten minutes, he swung his feet onto the ladder and climbed down quietly as the young mother watched. When his boots touched the floor, he turned and faced her, unsure what to do next. His tentativeness gave way and he slipped off his pack and knelt where his enemy had knelt. One hand held the pack and the other slid inside it, drawing out the powdered milk and the second candy bar. He placed them beside his enemy's music box. The mother nodded and smiled, and the soldier rose to leave. But at the door he stopped and looked back to the light, retraced his steps, and knelt again where his enemy had knelt.

The music box had run down. He picked it up. Solid but delicate, the work of a master. It was a fine gift. He wound it, opened the lid, and the waltz began.

The mother smiled. And when the hollow-eyed soldier looked toward the sleeping infant, she drew back the linen napkin to reveal its peaceful face.

Tears streamed down the soldier's cheeks. When the mother bowed her head, he closed his eyes and did the same. It was only a moment–a long moment in the midst of a long war–and when the young mother looked up, the hollow-eyed soldier was gone. Where he had knelt sat the music box playing its waltz. Draped across its open lid lay a beautiful, knitted shawl.

Neighbors

John Harner parks his car in his driveway and walks toward me, his lips moving as his hands illustrate. I throttle down the snow thrower so it's idling, but above its noisy blat-blatting I still can't make out what John is saying. At first I think he's thanking me for blowing a foot of snow from his sidewalk, which is no big deal. I'm lucky enough to own a reconditioned $40 yard-sale snow thrower which I run up and down both sides of our street. Many people here are older and shouldn't shovel.

"Haven't seen your dog in awhile," John says loudly, not quite shouting above the motor's noise. "Is he okay?" He's speaking of my pup Chooch, now ten months old and still chewing up my rugs.

"I've been keeping him inside or on the line in the back yard," I say, also just below a shout. John's face and mine are barely a foot apart.

John's a retired dentist. His wife died of cancer last spring, barely ten months after his retirement. There are still two cars in his driveway, and he makes sure both of them are exercised.

"I thought maybe something had happened to Chooch," John says.

"He's all right," I answer. "Well, all right now. Got run over a couple weeks ago."

I explain to John that the night it happened I'd let Chooch out to pee, and when I called him home he darted in front of a truck. Luckily the truck was a high-up four-wheel-drive, and Chooch is low to the ground, so its front bumper scraped his head and he got tumbled between the blacktop road and the truck's undercarriage like a load of wet wash in a clothes dryer, spitting him out the back. I saw the whole thing from the porch.

When the driver backed up to see what had happened, I assured him it wasn't his fault. Meanwhile Chooch disappeared. My wife and I searched until midnight, then went to bed for a fitful and guilty night's sleep, figuring Chooch had crawled off on this sub-zero night to die, either of his wounds or hypothermia. But he surprised us, showing up shivering on the back porch at breakfast time. After that night I'd kept him close, not allowing him to run alone. It had taken us two years from the death of our 14-year-old black Lab Otis before we felt ready to adopt Chooch.

"He's got two gouges up here," I say, pointing to the crown of my head. "Probably from the front bumper. It looks worse than it really is, because that's where the vet shaved him."

"Oh, thank God," John says, nodding.

The motor is still blatting, and I'm able to guess what John is saying by watching his lips. My ears pick up parts of his words. I wonder why he's still standing talking to me halfway out in the street as I'm running a snow thrower. It occurs to me that I've never seen John smile.

"I had to have them put Morgan down," he says. Morgan could have been the twin brother of our Otis, who carried box turtles home from the woods in his mouth, then played with them in the driveway like he was worrying a ham bone. My wife joked that at his age it was the only thing he could catch. Otis was the best dog we ever had. We loved him dearly, and having him put to sleep was the hardest thing we ever did.

"Morgan?" I spit out in disbelief. I hadn't known John's dog was sick.

"January twenty-fourth," he says. His lips draw tight together.

I try to figure out how long ago January twenty-fourth is, but the calculator part of my brain is numb. I rough it out at two, three, maybe four weeks. I'm deeply embarrassed that I haven't noticed him missing.

"He had cancer. The liver," John continues. His voice drops so that I can't actually hear the words, but I can see them coming off his lips. All I can see is John's pained eyes and his lips, as if there's a small square frame around them. I can't pull my eyes away.

"I didn't want him to suffer," he says, "So I had them do it before he got too bad."

It's hard to see behind the glare of John's glasses now, but I think he's tearing up. We've lived side by side all this time, but we've hardly spoken except for the chit-chat and small talk of people who occupy connecting house lots. No dinners together. No deep conversations. No borrowing rakes or hoes. Other than waving as we pull into our driveways or conversing briefly about our dogs, we don't know each other.

"He was a good, good dog," John says.

I feel my face responding, tightening into a prune of sympathy.

"Black Labs are great dogs," I say, and an image of

Otis with a mouthful of slimed turtle comes to mind. My eyes start to water. I'm tempted to shut off the snow thrower so we can freely talk about our grief, about our two dead 14 year-old black Labs. But then John might speak of his wife and I of my father, or the Town snowplow might need to get past us. I keep it running.

I ask, "So are you going to get another dog?" I kick myself as soon as the stupid words come out. I know damn well it's too soon. I'm angry and disappointed with myself for my insensitivity.

"I don't think so," John says. "Morgan was our second black Lab. John's tears are a frozen film over the lenses of his eyes. "We had each of them for 14 years. I don't want to go through it again." His face is a wall of pain.

I nod my head, but it's not enough. Or maybe it is, I don't know. I place my gloved hands back on the grips of the snow thrower.

Down the street I catch sight of the Town plow rounding our corner.

John sees it, too, and backs away from me onto his sidewalk. His voice grows louder as he says over the blat-blat, "Thanks for doing the sidewalks. Everyone on the street appreciates it." He catches me by surprise as he pulls his hand from his jacket pocket and thrusts it in my direction. I remove my glove and shake his bare hand. It's a long handshake, and he's looking me straight in the eye as he squeezes. A wave of thanks would have sufficed. John releases his grip, and I mine. He turns and walks back toward his other car, the one his wife always drove.

I drop the snow thrower into gear, throttle up, and move on to clear my own driveway. In the dining room window I can see Chooch, forepaws on the window sill, nose breath making a cloud on the icy glass, watching me work.

Peevil's Eyebrow

Peevil Wainwright was the kid in our class with the extra eyebrow. Perfectly formed, it ran parallel above his left one. Upon meeting him for the first time, people who didn't know Peevil often tried to warn him that a caterpillar was stuck to his forehead. He shaved it for awhile, but he was forever cutting the skin because it was so thin and tender beneath the eyebrow. Even when he did shave it, it left first a pale patch, then a dark shadow as it came back.

Those of us who grew up with Peevil got used to it, as any group gets used to a member with a missing finger, birthmark, or limp. Sure, we'd kid him, saying things like, "It moved!" or "It crawled!" or "Look. It was on the right side yesterday, but now it's on the left!" But that's because we were *compadres.* Peevil learned to laugh and make jokes about it himself, especially with newcomers. (Highbrow humor, he called it.)

"Oh," he'd say, "Did I misplace my Hitler mustache again?" Or, "Where'd that caterpillar go? I hate it when it spins a cocoon while I'm asleep with my mouth open. Then I wake up and my stomach is all butterflies."

The most fun was at baseball games. Peevil was our catcher, so he'd wear a mask much of the game. He'd wait until a batter had a couple of men on base, then, just before the pitch, he'd ask the umpire for time-out to adjust his mask. He'd take it off face-to-face with the batter, then put it back on. Often as not, the batter would take a standing strike three, still thinking about that third eyebrow. We called it "giving them the Peevil eye."

Peevil couldn't wiggle the third eyebrow apart from the other two. He could wiggle each of the normal ones alone, without moving the extra. But if he wiggled the one below the extra vigorously, or the two normal eyebrows together, that upper one would jump, too. It was comical to see, and he forever made us laugh in classes–wiggling the caterpillar when the teacher wasn't looking, then pretending to be innocent while the rest of us got detention for giggling.

One Halloween, Peevil drew a fourth eyebrow above the single right one, then added an eye, a third eye, dead-center above the bridge of his nose. Somehow four eyebrows didn't seem as unusual as three, not on Halloween, and the third eye drew all the attention anyway. He dressed as a vampire, and at each house he'd say in his best Bela Lugosi Transylvanian accent, "My mother said to keep an eye out crossing the street." It didn't make perfect sense, but for once it helped keep the attention off Peevil's extra eyebrow.

At seventeen Peevil he got a job driving a *Good Humor* ice cream truck on the other side of town where folks didn't know him. He wore a *Good Humor* cap, so the shadow of its brim pretty much hid the eyebrow.

But one steaming hot day, as a crowd of little kids clamored for popsicles, he took his cap off to wipe his forehead. The kids stared at him as if he'd stepped out of a *Twilight Zone* episode, and two of them screamed. The whole crowd joined in and it became self-fed hysteria. Parents streamed off porches, fearing their children had stumbled upon nests of angry hornets. But Peevil had his cap pulled tight over his forehead by then, and the children, all quite young, could only point and babble. None could clearly describe the cause of their fright. Peevil shrugged and appeared bewildered.

When everyone turned to leave, a couple of kids looked back. Sensing an encore, Peevil tipped his cap and wiggled all three eyebrows. The kids screamed, but the cap was in place when the parents turned around. Peevil shook his head as if he hadn't a clue.

"Can't you have it removed surgically?" my sister Cassie asked Peevil in junior high. Many others had asked the same question, though I never did.

"The doctor said it'd be too expensive," Peevil answered. "Besides, my Dad said it'd just be taking off layers of skin, but the hairs would grow back."

"Like perennials," Cassie said, bringing some of her newfound, seventh-grade science knowledge to the conversation.

"Something like that," Peevil said.

"Or crabgrass," Jimmy Pardoner added.

Peevil laughed with Jimmy and the rest of us at the joke. Cassie didn't laugh.

The eyebrow kept him out of the service, too, at a time when many of our classmates were going to Viet Nam. Peevil truly wanted to do his part, but the Army doctors said no. Their disqualifications list included such disabilities as blindness and flat feet, but not extra eyebrows, but they ruled Peevil 4F, ineligible, a decision he appealed.

"Think how distracted the generals would be when

I saluted them," Peevil joked after the appeal was rejected. We all laughed, but Cassie said being rejected by the Army hurt his feelings and his jokes were a cover-up.

"Maybe," I said. "But I think Peevil can laugh at himself."

"Easy for you to say," she snapped. "You've only got two eyebrows!"

As she stomped away I found I felt guilty that I had only two eyebrows. Not only guilty, but something about the fierce way my sister defended him made me feel jealous. I wanted an extra eyebrow.

That night I dreamed I was caught in an English garden, lost in a maze of hedges. Eventually, I found a tree in the middle and climbed it.. I could see there was no escape, no way out. Far off, at the outer edge, a gardener stood working with hedge clippers, scissoring away. "Hey," I yelled. "Cut an opening so I can get out. I'm trapped. The gardener yelled back, "I can't. It grows back as fast as I trim it." Then, laughing like a madman, he disappeared behind the hedge.

Cassie married Jeff when she was twenty. He'd been a football player at a nearby college and she'd met him in the college cafeteria. She got pregnant right after the wedding, about the same time Jeff flunked out and joined the Army. The plan was for Cassie to join Jeff after boot camp and have the baby at an Army hospital. But in boot camp, while doing calisthenics on a hot day, Jeff dropped dead of heart failure. In the midst of her grief, and while living at home with Mom and Dad, Cassie had the baby. She named him Derrick.

I was away at college, but I saw my sister and my new nephew Derrick on vacations. I thought Cassie would never get beyond the pain of Jeff's death.

But in my senior year of college, on the first morning home for spring break, the doorbell rang and I answered it. There stood Peevil Wainwright whom I hadn't seen since graduation. I'd headed to college; he'd joined his father in the hardware business. He'd brought along the old pet caterpillar, which I half-expected him to wiggle to make me laugh. But he didn't. He simply stood there.

"Can I come in?" he asked politely.

"Uh, oh, sure, Peeve," I hemmed. "Sorry. Come in."

Peevil stepped inside.

"What's doin'?" I asked.

"Cassie here?" he asked, as if he hadn't heard my question at all. He looked beyond me.

"Cassie?" I asked. Peevil had always hung around with me. "Uh, well, let me get her. Wait here." I walked to the stairs and yelled up, "Cass? Cass? Somebody here to see you."

Peevil stood straight and tall, and I noticed he had a sport coat on. No tie, just a light blue shirt, tan pants, and a Navy blue sport coat. No hat. It struck me how much he looked like a man.

"Hi, Peeve," I heard Cassie's voice say from the top of the stairs. I saw she had Derrick on her hip, a pacifier in his mouth.

"Hi, Cass," Peevil said, a broad smile appearing.

Cassie started down the stairs. I watched him watch her, as if she were a princess descending a marble staircase. And then I saw it. Peevil Wainwright, Evil Peevil, the class clown, was in love. Peevil, the catcher, the vampire, the *Good Humor* man, the rejected soldier, the young man who knew pain and the many unfairnesses of life, who had learned compassion by experience, was in love with my sister Cassie.

And she, so numb, so inconsolable, was in love with him. My sister loved Peevil Wainwright, the freak of nature, the kid with three eyebrows. And when I saw her smile, saw her glow, saw her wholeness as she walked to greet him, I loved him myself. I loved that Peevil Wainwright. I loved him then and there and for all time, and I wanted to run and kiss him, by God, wanted to run and kiss him on that lovely, lovely eyebrow.

The Ice Fisherman

Cornelia watched from her parlor window, waiting for her brother Paul to appear on the frozen lake. He always walked onto the ice from behind the pines that made up the boundary between her land and his. They'd lived there all their lives–she, at seventy, occupying the family homestead she'd inherited thirty years earlier, and he, at sixty-eight, in his log cabin on the land their father had given him when Paul came back disabled from the war in Europe in 1945.

A dozen fishing shacks dotted the ice near the middle of the lake. Paul's was the light green one with the fluorescent orange door. Six or eight more fishing shacks–shanties, some folks called them–rested on the far shore on dry ground. Their owners either hadn't gotten them on the ice for the winter or had begun pulling them off early, anticipating an early thaw.

Paul's shack had been a more conservative color when he inherited it from their father, a dull brown, weathered with age. Except for the three years when her brother was away in the Navy and the year of his recuperation (not just from the physical recuperation but getting over the nightmares, one of which he claimed had begun recurring again recently after a forty year hiatus), Paul hadn't missed a winter of ice fishing on the lake since he was six. Fifty-eight years of fishing.

A snowmobile crossed the lake, coming first as a speck from the far shore where two dozen year-round camps had sprung up. There had been only two when Cornelia and Paul were growing up–one Uncle Freeman's, the other a rental cabin–and those used only in summer.

From behind the thermal-paned window Cornelia couldn't hear the whine of the snowmobile. Fine with her. She agreed with Paul that snowmobile racket shattered the peace of the place. Cross-country skiing was all right, but not noisy snow-mobiling. Peace was what Paul loved more than anything, a sense of peace.

The snowmobile crossed the center point of the lake, weaving its way among ice fishing shacks as if negotiating an obstacle course. Once through the maze, it sped toward Cornelia's small dock. The driver was a boy–what, nine or ten–too young, she thought, to be riding the dangerous machine alone. She could hear their mother's voice railing against the evils of motorcycles in the 1930's, when Paul bought an old "hog" for the dirt roads between Lake Elmore and Montpelier.

"You be careful, Paul" Cornelia could hear her mother cautioning. "I want you home for supper in one piece."

The snowmobile slowed and veered before reaching the dock, then cruised parallel to the shore as if on drill parade. When the boy's hand went up in a wave, Cornelia's hand started up, too, in answer, but then she saw that Paul had emerged from the pines and was waving at the boy. A shadow crossed the ice between them–clouds overhead, no doubt–and Paul continued on toward his shack as the snowmobile kept following the shoreline and grew smaller.

Paul made his usual bee-line for the orange-doored shanty, pulling his ancient Flexible Flyer sled behind him. He limped in his usual way, first on his good leg with the insulated engineer's boot, then on the wooden one, mahogany from the knee down, saw-toothed heel plate on the end of the peg so it'd bite into the ice. He'd hobbled to his ice fishing shack thousands of times that way.

Cornelia smiled and shook her head as she thought once more of the irony. Paul's ship had been sunk in the North Atlantic by a German sub, and he'd had to adapt to a wooden leg. Yet here she sat day after day with two legs, each weak and unsteady, while her brother trekked onto the lake daily to fish.

Paul turned, looked Cornelia's way, waved. She returned it, their daily visual litany, a comfort. Only today's wave–what was there about it? Perhaps a heaviness, a tiredness she sensed rather than saw?

Her brother had never married. Cornelia had, but her husband Rudy has passed on fifteen years earlier. They'd never had children. Now it was just her and her brother.

Paul stood outside his shack, near where the white ice turned greenish-blue. A spring fed it from below, which was why Paul set his shack there year after year. Their father had said the Abenaki Indians believed the swirling spring was made up of spirits. Paul didn't know about that, he simply claimed the spring made it the best part of the lake for fishing.

"Springs are life-giving," he said. "Like circulating your blood."

She watched him disappear inside. It wasn't cold; in fact, the sun was bright and the lake's surface had been warming for days. Cornelia knew Paul wouldn't light the kerosene heater he kept inside the shack.

She knew her brother's routine, could picture him unfolding and setting up the blue canvas director's chair he kept on a nail. He'd use the rusty hatchet to break up any new ice that had formed over the hole in the night. Then he'd drop in his lines, settle back in the chair, and reach for the well-chewed cigar in the pewter ashtray on the shelf. He'd work the cigar around until it fit his lips and teeth with the snugness of a marble settling into a hole on a Chinese Checkers board. He never smoked the cigar, didn't even chew it. Just held it there in his mouth most of the morning and afternoon, removing it only to eat the sandwich and cookies in his lunchbox. When he left at mid-afternoon, he'd rest the cigar in its cradle on the lip of the pewter ashtray for next time.

"Don't hurt me if I don't smoke it," Paul would argue whenever she and Rudy had kidded him about the cigar. "Besides, unsmoked, a good cigar will last a week, maybe two."

Paul hadn't actually smoked a cigar since the day Kennedy died in Dallas, and he never said why he'd quit then. Unless he'd told Rudy, that is, Rudy who'd been not only his brother-in-law but his best friend. But if he had told Rudy, Rudy had taken the secret to his grave with him.

The sun cleared the peak to the east, and the thermometer outside Cornelia's parlor window read forty degrees. If it got much warmer and stayed that way, the ice above the springs would soften. It was already beginning to melt around the edges of the lake.

Cornelia felt a seed of worry. She'd seen it happen before, the melt above the spring. Shacks sank into the ice as if in quicksand, tilting this way and that. Sometimes the lake would refreeze and the owners wouldn't be able to free them. Or if the shacks sank at final thaw of the season, they'd wait a month or two and retrieve them by boat, towing them home like dead whales.

Paul's had sunk only once, when he and Rudy had driven to Virginia for a Navy reunion. Things had warmed up unexpectedly. She could still remember how it chilled her to watch the coffin-shaped shanty sink gradually into the ice over those four days. In the end, only the roof was visible.

"I can always get another cigar," Paul had joked upon his return from Virginia, when he discovered the submerged shack.

Cornelia had wondered if it didn't remind him of the war and his ship's sinking, after which he and a group of his shipmates had spent two days adrift. Everyone but Paul had eventually slipped into the icy waters while awaiting rescue. Frostbite had claimed his leg and several fingers. He'd been decorated but insisted he didn't deserve to get the same medal the others got, which was why Cornelia kept the framed medal on her wall. Paul wouldn't allow it in his house. He spoke to no one about the sinking or his comrades' fate except Rudy, who confided to Cornelia that he thought Paul carried a load of unnecessary guilt.

The boy on the snowmobile zipped along the far shore, drove up the bank to a small frame house with smoke trailing from its chimney, and disappeared inside. Could he be done for the day? It was barely 9:30.

Another fisherman appeared three cabins east of

the snowmobiler, wearing an insulated coverall outfit, fluorescent pink with black trim. If he hadn't walked toward a shanty, Cornelia would have thought him a jogger. He disappeared inside the shack farthest from Paul's. The sun felt warm streaming through the window and made Cornelia sleepy.

The Regulator clock above the piano read one-thirty when she awoke. The sunlight that had put her to sleep had moved around to the other side of the house, and she felt cold. She moved to the kitchen for tea and a jelly sandwich, spreading butter on the bread before applying jelly, the way their mother had always done it. Paul had done it that way, too, until his heart problem, so now he skipped the butter.

"Hard to believe," he had said in honest disbelief. "A bum ticker. How can that be, with all the fish I eat?" Nevertheless, he had heeded his doctor, cut down on his fat, and lost weight. It was all he could do, since he wasn't a good candidate for bypass surgery.

Cornelia returned to the parlor window, sweater around her shoulders, lap blanket over her knees. Forty-eight degrees outside, and that from a thermometer reading in the shade. A gnawing returned to her stomach. She sipped her tea to calm it, and as she looked up from her tea cup–just for a second, the briefest moment–she was sure she saw Paul's friends standing together and looking at her, smiling, from a distance. She swallowed hard, almost choked, then she realized it was a reflection she was seeing in the window, a reflection of the World War II black-and-white photograph of Paul and his buddies that sat on the small table behind her. Except that Paul was in the photograph behind her. Had he been in the reflection she'd mistaken for the gathered group on the lake?

The jogging-suit fisherman stepped from his shanty and started the walk home. A string of small fish dangled from his hand. His free hand went up in a wave, and Cornelia saw that the snowmobiler had come back onto the lake and was waving. The boy showed a burst of speed the way young boys did in front of men, then headed straight across the lake toward her, bisecting it. From so far away, he resembled a teardrop dripping down her windowpane.

He turned the machine and put it into a skid before reaching Cornelia's shoreline, spitting up ice shavings as a figure skater did upon pulling up short. As he did, she felt the tiniest breath of air, chill air. A draft through a tightly shut window? It caressed her cheeks and a frisson of dread tingled along her spine. She drew her sweater tighter around her. Then the boy was flying across the ice again the way Cornelia had seen her father do sixty years earlier in his iceboat. This machine seemed less graceful, less fluid.

Paul stepped from his shack, stretched like someone awaking from a nap. He glanced toward Cornelia, then reached back in and pulled out a double string of fish, ten or a dozen. He held the strings up as if he were an Olympic athlete displaying a medal.

Cornelia smiled. So did Paul, and for the first time ever she caught a glimpse of sunshine reflecting off his gold-capped eye tooth. She was amazed to think she could see it at that distance. Was it because he hadn't smiled that broadly in awhile, or that the sun and the angle had never been right? It reminded her of an old movie she'd seen, where the hero's eyes and smile had flashed from the screen. Her brother, the hero.

That's when the snowmobile crashed through the ice. The boy went down, clutching the controls of the heavy machine. It never floated, not even for a moment, something it might have done had it been a four-wheeler with air in the tires. This was all metal and treads, and it simply disappeared down toward the bottom where the spring fed in. He must have let go the controls once he was underwater, and his snowmobile suit, perhaps because of the air trapped inside it, buoyed him to the surface. He thrashed his arms. Cornelia could see his mouth opening and closing, but she heard nothing. Her eyes searched the far shore for the jogging-suit fisherman. He was gone, probably in his cabin.

She saw Paul hobbling fast toward the boy, booted foot on his good leg slipping, metal-toothed heel on the wooden peg gripping, biting the ice. Fifty yards to the boy, but Paul was closing the gap fast. The boy foundered and the snowmobile suit that had buoyed him now took on water, changing from life preserver to anchor.

The pink and black fisherman appeared in his doorway, perhaps to retrieve the fish from his porch. He glanced at the lake, dropped his fish, and broke into a run. He had two hundred yards to cover.

Paul was almost to the boy now, dragging his Flexible Flyer sled. He pulled up short of the ice break, swung the sled the way a mule-skinner side-arms a whip. The sled snapped toward the hole and splashed into the water in front of the boy's outstretched arms.

"Grab it!" Cornelia screamed. But the boy was too panicked and continued thrashing wildly. She pounded the window sill, yelled again, "The sled! Grab the sled!"

The man in pink and black looked like a runner now. A hundred yards to cover. Cornelia could see his mouth moving.

The boy flapped his arms twice more, looking the last time as if his hand might strike and grasp one of the runners of the sled. But the icy water turned his clothing to lead. He went under.

Paul let go the sled rope, planted his metal-tipped wooden leg as a pole vaulter plants the pole at take-off, and catapulted into the opening. Cornelia screamed as her brother vanished beneath the surface. The other fisherman reached the hole and stood staring blankly into it. Cornelia held her breath.

Suddenly the slushy water exploded as a head broke the surface. Two heads. In the midst of that upward-thrusting, breaching-whale motion Paul's strong arms heaved the boy out and onto the ice. The man in pink and black clutched the boy, then dragged him back from the hole. Paul rested his arms on the edge of the ice, and Cornelia saw him smile. The sun caught the gold-capped tooth again as he glanced her way. A second later she glimpsed the pain, the excruciating pain, as Paul's face contorted. His heart.

The other fisherman could do nothing.

Cornelia could do nothing. Then she saw Paul's hand come up–a salute perhaps–before his face relaxed and he slipped backward, backward into the icy water with his comrades, into the chilly sleep. She couldn't see him, but somehow she wasn't afraid either. She could picture him–drifting, drifting slowly downward, like a leaf in autumn, freed from the tree, drifting slowly downward into his comrades' open arms, drifting downward to rest, to rest in the life-giving spring.

The Trellis

Never was a floor scoured whiter than the floor in the long dark kitchen at Grandma and Grandpa Freeman's. It was a bare floor, unpainted and unwaxed, but it was scrubbed until it looked as soft as the grass.

The farmhouse was old, built around the middle of the nineteenth century, and Grandma and Grandpa seemed to me to have been set in there along with the cornerstone. Their living room was always cheery, with its bright rag rug and dancing, popping fire in the fireplace. Grandma had the brass globes on top of the andirons polished so shiny that the firelight fairly ricocheted around the room before it reached my eyes. But most of the warmth came from Grandma and Grandpa, for they talked about what I wanted to talk about and listened to what I had to say.

Grandma knew before I did when I was thinking about cookies.

And Grandpa mus*t* have fixed 50 bicycle tires for me. He called bicycles *wheels.*

"If you'll bring your wheel over after school, I'll tighten the seat up for you," he'd say.

Whenever Grandpa made a little joke about Grandma's cooking, he'd twinkle his eye at me and wink so Grandma could see it. She'd punch him lightly on the arm or shoulder and scowl a mock scowl as if irritated. Then she'd kind of coo, "Oh, Pop." Together, they were the cornerstones of the house.

The last time I saw them was when I went away to college. They held a little outdoor tea for my sister and me.

My sister and I had spent a good part of our youth there, traipsing through the woods and up and down the hillsides. We'd comb the pasturelands for nuts and wild strawberries. Of course, we were also always on the alert for wild boars, prowling Bengal tigers, dinosaurs, and New England's dreaded rogue elephants. We often watched herds of ferocious beasts crossing the crocodile-infested streams.

The tea party wasn't a somber occasion, it was fun. What I remember about it, though, isn't the party but the rose trellis. Unpainted and weathered, it was simply two ladder-like sections of an old picket fence, now leaned together. The thorny vines of two rose bushes twined in and out through the pickets and embraced each other at the top. It looked like an "A" without a crossbar. I always thought it should be nailed to keep it together, but Grandpa disagreed. So it never got nailed.

Grandma died during my sophomore year of college. A stroke. Grandpa never recovered from the loss, and he joined her three months later. I wanted to make it to the funerals, but I couldn't get away for either one. Maybe I just couldn't face it. They left me the old farmhouse, but I had to leave it empty while I finished college and grad school. It was five years before I could get back there.

When my new wife and I paid our first visit to the old homestead, it was plain that nothing had changed. Yet everything looked and felt different. The rooms were cobwebbed and the floors dark and dusty. Only charred logs and gray ashes lay in the silent fireplace, and my eyes barely noticed the tarnished andirons standing in the shadow of the cold hearth. The rag rug appeared faded, though it was probably mostly dust. Now frayed, it was beginning to unravel.

The back yard, where Grandma and Grandpa had hosted my farewell tea, lay choked and overgrown with dusty rye grass. But for a moment I could picture my grandparents sitting there in their lawn chairs. My eyes filled up and the distant hillsides blurred.

I stumbled. Something underfoot that I'd missed seeing.

There in the high weeds lay the fallen trellis, one section lying atop the other. I had told Grandpa it would fall some day.

As I stared at the pickets, I recalled the rose bushes. My wife knelt beside me. With a brush of her skirt she swept the dirt from the trellis, looked into my face, and smiled, a soft smile, like Grandma used to smile. Together we straightened up the trellis, propping its two ladder-like sections against each other as they had once been, like an "A" without a crossbar.

We never nailed it. Never had to. The two rose bushes we planted twined through the pickets and embraced at the top.

The trellis stands there today.

The Magi's Gift

Matthew looked at the clock for the umpteenth time. Six-fifteen. Only a little over an hour until pageant time. Granny Howell had said he could leave at six-thirty. Matthew was itching to go.

One year he'd played Joseph, Jesus' father. Another year he'd played an angel, with a coat hanger halo that kept bouncing and hitting him on the forehead and tin foil wings that were forever brushing against the piano or against the church flag in the small chancel area. In kindergarten he'd played a donkey, which was a step up from the previous year when he'd been a sheep. When he was a first-grader he played a shepherd. His mother had been alive then, and she and Granny had never tired of telling how Matthew and his cousin Freddy (also a shepherd) nearly poked out the Dennis sisters' eyes by nervously wobbling and tapping their shepherds' crooks. The two honey-voiced teens had gotten to laughing so hysterically they couldn't finish their duet. Matthew thought that he remembered it, but he wasn't really sure, because it might be the retellings he was recalling.

This year would be his first chance to try a new part, a Magi, one of the three wise kings from the East. Matthew was excited, because the Magi were the best dressed in the cast (if you didn't count angels as being well dressed, which he didn't) and the Magi got to deliver gifts. The robes were surely better than Mary's and Joseph's clothing, and much sharper looking than the dusty shepherds' garb. Besides, Granny Howell had bought a nice gold terry cloth bathrobe for the occasion, one with his initials–MPW–monogrammed on the breast. The robe would look like a true king's finery and, after its pageant duty, it would prove very warm on New England's cold winter nights.

"Here's the candle, Matthew," Granny Howell said, handing him a candle the size of a coffee can. "Don't forget to say your mother's name when you light it from the altar candle."

The candle was a blend of many colors. It was no mistake that it was the size and shape of a coffee can, because throughout the year Matthew and his grandmother had saved the stubs from dozens of different colored candles and melted them together to make one great rainbow candle. The church's tradition was to include a brief time at the end of the Nativity Pageant when parishioners could light candles they'd brought along in memory of loved ones, then set them around the manger area. Last year had been the first time Matthew and Granny Howell had made a rainbow candle and lit it in memory of Matthew's mother, Granny's daughter. Granny called it "a candle of hope, like the rainbow Noah saw from the ark." They'd lit it together then, but this year, with Granny wheelchair-bound and recovering from a broken hip after a Thanksgiving fall, Matthew was going to church alone to light the candle for both of them.

"It smells good, Granny," Matthew said, holding the candle under his nose.

"It's that cinnamon we put in," she said. "I told you it would give a lovely smell. It's how your Mom and I used to make them when she was your age."

Matthew nodded and smiled. It was hard for him to imagine his mother as a child his age.

The hallway clock struck once. Six-thirty. Time to go.

Matthew opened the door.

"Got everything?" Granny asked, offering a check-list the way she did in the morning when Matthew was heading off to school.

"Bathrobe?"

"Check."

"Candle?"

"Check."

"Cookies?"

"Che–" Matthew stopped mid-word. He'd forgotten the tollhouse cookies Granny had baked especially for Reverend Tyler. Matthew and Granny both liked him a lot. He had conducted Matthew's mom's funeral. The cookies were still on the kitchen table. Matthew ran to get them. They were wrapped in aluminum foil inside a beautifully decorated maroon and silver fruit-cake tin. Matthew was to give the cookies to Reverend Tyler as a Christmas gift, then use the expensive-looking container as his Magi prop for the Nativity Pageant. He would bend with a noble bow and leave the tin at the feet of the Christ child as his kingly gift. Matthew returned to the front hallway pretending to be out of breath from his mad dash to the kitchen.

"Check!" he said with a broad grin on his face, cookie tin in front of him. "Bathrobe, candle, cookies." He worked the thick candle into his coat pocket, folded the bathrobe and slid it into a rope-handled Macy's shopping bag, and placed the cookie tin in the bag on top of the bathrobe. He kissed Granny Howell and she waved goodbye from her wheelchair.

"Don't dawdle, Matthew," she called after him. "You go straight to church, Matthew." Granny Howell knew her grandson's ways. He was a lot like his mother had been.

The evening air was chilly and the slight breeze bit into Matthew's skin. A few large, clean snowflakes drifted lazily downward, seeming to come from the streetlights above. One landed on Matthew's nose. He stuck out his tongue to catch the coldness of another. It reminded him of the cold snow that had flown in his face one night his mother had taken him sledding at Pucker's Hill. They had placed a kerosene lantern at the top of the hill, another halfway down, and a third at the bottom.

Matthew passed the cedar-shingled blacksmith shop that was falling down. It was a small barn more than a hundred years old; it hadn't been used as a blacksmith shop in twenty years. Its roof leaked and was beginning to cave in near the back, and most of the windows were broken out. But it hadn't been torn down, because the old blacksmith was ninety-five and still alive in a nursing home. All the good tools had long since been looted. No one took care of the place and no one wanted to be a blacksmith, so the shop fell into disrepair.

Matthew noticed a rough handmade wreath on the heavy garage door in front. He drifted closer and peered through a broken-paned window. Inside glowed a light. A man stood warming his hands over a small bed of coals in the old forge. He hummed something, but Matthew couldn't make out the tune or the words. The man caught sight of Matthew.

"Merry Christmas," the man said. He continued to warm his hands.

"Merry Christmas," Matthew answered. "Whatcha doin'?"

"Keepin' warm."

"In the blacksmith shop?" Even though he'd never seen the building used for its original purpose? Matthew knew what a blacksmith did, and he knew the building was still referred to by local people as the blacksmith shop.

"Yup. I live here sometimes."

"Why?"

"Gotta live somewhere."

Now Matthew recognized him. He was the odd-jobs man everyone called Dusty. Matthew didn't know his real name, but he did know Granny Howell had hired him to rake the leaves in the yard a few times. And he'd painted the fence. Some of the kids were scared of him and called him Cyclops, because he had only one good eye. The bad one was a dead, milky color.

"You're Dusty, aren't you?" Matthew asked.

"Yup," the man replied. "And yourself?"

"Matthew Wilder. You painted my Granny Howell's fence." Matthew noticed the man had two flannel shirts on. Behind him, in a corner lit by a candle that sat flickering on a saucer, was a cot with a pile of blankets on it.

"That must have been two summers ago," Dusty said. "Was that you sitting there watching me from the porch?"

"That was me." Matthew could see, even in the dim light, that Dusty's eyebrows were thick and almost connected to his wild beard. He wore a Russian Cossack hat on his head.

The two of them were silent for a moment.

"Was it your mother who died, then? Sometime in the fall after I painted the fence?"

"Yeah," Matthew answered. "She was sick a whole year."

"I'm sorry," Dusty answered. "It must be hard for you."

"Yeah," Matthew said.

Another moment of silence.

When Matthew didn't move away from the window, Dusty said, "Cold enough for ya?"

"Oh, you bet," Matthew answered, perking up. "Must be cold in here at night, huh?"

"Well, sometimes. Not too bad at the moment. I keep using what's left of the old blacksmith's soft coal in this forge. It keeps the chill off. I can't complain."

"You make the wreath?" Matthew asked, still from outside the door, looking through the broken window.

"Yup."

"It's nice."

Silence again.

"I'm on my way to church, to the pageant. You going?"

"Nah. I'm not much on church. Besides, the fire'd go out."

"I suppose. Well, I gotta go. I'm a king this year."

"Have a good time."

"I will. See ya, Mr. Dusty."

"Dusty is fine, son. You can call me Dusty."

"Okay, see ya, Dusty."

"Goodbye, Matthew."

Matthew started to turn away, then turned back and asked through the broken window pane, "Would you like some Christmas cookies, Dusty? They're tollhouse. My Granny Howell made 'em." Before the man inside could answer, Matthew had set his Macy's shopping bag down, removed the maroon and silver cookie tin from atop the gold bathrobe, popped the tin top, and lifted out the foil-wrapped cookies. He pushed open the huge door and stepped inside. "Here," he said, presenting the cookies to the man.

Dusty reached out and placed his hands under the cookies. "Thanks," he said with a smile that revealed the wrinkle lines under his good eye and under his milky eye.

Matthew's fingers brushed Dusty's as he handed over the cookies. He could feel the warmth of the man's rough, coal-warmed hands. "You're welcome," said Matthew with a nod.

The candle by the cot flickered. Dusty cast a backward glance at it. There was nothing left but a shimmering pool of wax and the gasping tip of a wick. It flickered again.

"The draft," Matthew said. "I'd better close the door." He turned to leave, and as he did he felt the heavy rainbow candle in his pocket clunk against his hip. He slid his hand into his pocket to steady it.

"Awful glad you came, Matthew," the man said.

Matthew looked back at the large, bearded man in the blacksmith shop. Clad in two flannel shirts and a Russian hat, a smile on his face and a clutch of twinkling, foil-wrapped cookies resting on his palms in front of him, he looked like a king, a Magi bearing a gift. The waxy candle in Matthew's pocket felt warm and soft.

"Would a bathrobe help you keep warm?" Matthew asked. "I've got one with me, you know, in my shopping bag." The boy's eyes searched the man's face.

"I've got clothes aplenty, thank you," Dusty said. "As you can see, I'm wearing two shirts at a time now. And there's plenty of blankets on the bed." Dusty lifted a hand and pointed at the cot in the corner. The candle flickered again but didn't go out.

Matthew's eyes turned downward. His fingers wrapped themselves tightly around the warm candle in his pocket. He turned once more to leave and pushed the door open more, enough to get though. The fingers of his left hand caught up the Macy's bag and his feet started toward the church. But his heart won out and he spun around and knocked on the heavy door. "Dusty?" he called.

"Come in," said a muffled voice from inside.

Matthew opened the door and saw that Dusty was already sitting down on his cot, eating the tollhouse cookies. He looked up as the boy crossed the firelit room toward him, shopping bag on his left arm, right arm pulling something from his coat pocket.

"Here's one that won't burn out for a long, long time," Matthew said. He handed Dusty his mother's coffee-can-sized rainbow candle. "Merry Christmas."

Cookie in mouth, Dusty mumbled "Merry Chriffmuff" and watched Matthew once more disappear into the streetlights and the huge, lazy, drifting snowflakes.

Perfect, Just Perfect

It was four days before Christmas, and no sign of snow in the air. Everything in town lay still, as if Old Man Winter had forgotten the snow everyone was wishing for. Grampa and I were working at the department store. He was Santa Claus and I was his helper. He did the ho-hoing and asked kids what they wanted for Christmas. I was the candy-cane-and-present-passer-outer. Our hours were from four until seven-thirty.

Grampa's beard was real. Some of the kids who tugged it were quite surprised. It wasn't pure white, but it was bushy and full. When Grampa ho-hoed, his stomach shook. He was Santa Claus, no question.

Most of the lap-sitters were under ten. They were pretty much alike, asking for bikes, dolls, radios, and games.

But one little girl was different. Her mother brought her up, and Grampa hoisted her onto his lap. Her name was Tina. She was blind.

"What do you want for Christmas, Tina?" Grampa asked.

"Snow," she answered shyly.

Grampa smiled. His eyes twinkled. "We'll see what we can do about that. But how about something for you, yourself? Something special?"

Tina hesitated, then whispered something in

Grandpa's ear. I couldn't hear her words, but I saw a smile creep over Grampa's face.

"Sure, Tina," was all he said.

He took her hands in his and placed them on his cheeks. His eyes closed and he sat there smiling as the girl began to sculpt his face with her fingers. She paused here and there to linger, paying close attention to every wrinkle and whisker. She seemed to be memorizing with her fingers the laugh lines under Grampa's eyes and at the corners of his mouth. She stroked his beard and rolled its wiry ringlets between her thumbs and forefingers. When she finished, she paused to rest her palms on Grampa's shoulders.

He opened his eyes. They were twinkling.

Suddenly her arms flew out, encircling Grampa's neck in a crushing hug.

"Oh, Santa," she cried. "You look just like I knew you. You're perfect, just perfect."

As Tina's mother lifted her down from his lap, Grampa turned his head toward me. He smiled, then blinked, and a tear rolled down his cheek.

That night when my grandmother came to pick us up, I watched her help Grampa shift over from the Santa chair into his wheelchair. As she was positioning his limp legs on the foot rests, she said, "So, Santa, how was your day?"

He looked up at me and pressed his lips together. Then he looked down at Gramma, cleared his throat, and said with a tiny smile, "Sweetheart, it was perfect. Just perfect."

Outside it began to snow.

Garden by the River

"Honest to God, to this day I don't know if it was my imagination or real. But it sure'n heck turned my hair white forty years too soon."

The words caught ten year-old Todd's attention. He was visiting his uncle's Vermont hill farm on the Back River Road and had been standing in front of the potato chips, making a selection, when he overheard the three old-timers swapping stories.

They were all in their seventies or eighties, Todd guessed, sitting in rockers. It was obvious that the back corner of Harlow's General Store was a regular meeting place for them.

"I was eleven at the time ..."

Todd located the storyteller. His hair was white, not gray but white. Todd's jaw slackened and he moved closer as the old man continued his story.

"Yes, I was about the age of that young lad," he said, pointing to Todd. One of the other men had a bushy, wiry beard and gold-framed glasses that reminded Todd of a Christmas poster. He used his foot to nudge a chair toward Todd.

Todd sat down.

"Back then I lived with my Grandpa and Grandma on their farm, out on the Back River Road. Everybody called it the Injun Path back then, because there had been a couple of Indian settlements there around the time of the Revolution. Grandpa said they were always turning up arrowheads in the fields after a hard rain or after plowing.

"That summer I'd walk the Injun Path every day when I went to town for the mail or to pick up a can of tobacco for Grandpa. It was two or three miles to town.

"A woman lived out on the Injun Path, halfway between Grandpa's and town. Grandpa said she was descended on the one side from the Abenaki Indians and on the other side from runaway slaves. I don't know if it was true, but she was different, kind of queer, standoffish. Nobody I talked to had ever seen her face.

"She spent all her time tending a garden on the back corner of her property, a piece of river bottomland where the river oxbows and the land's shaped like a thumb. The garden had a low stone wall around it and a tall scarecrow in the middle. Grandpa said every year that woman would shine a couple of pie tins and hang them from the wrists of her scarecrow. We'd see the sun glint off them whenever we went by.

"Something else, too. No matter how hot it was, that woman'd always wear dark clothing. Yessir, dark clothing and a black veil–like a hood. She'd cover her head with it so you couldn't see her face. Grandpa said she was superstitious and wore it to ward off the spirit-stealers. They can only possess you by looking you in the eye, you know. Then your soul's theirs. Grandpa also said it was a known fact that spirit-stealers couldn't cross water.

"Well, not long before that the Congregational Church hired a new minister, Reverend Evans. He made a lot of enemies in a short time. I sort of liked him, though, maybe because my own father died when I was young. See him in his black suit and that black broad-brimmed hat, you'd figure him for Ichabod Crane.

"Grandma took me to church with her a few times, but only once did Grandpa come along. She believed you should go whether you liked the minister or not, and many times said, 'Go to church through thick and thin, or heaven'll come and you'll not get in.' Grandpa disagreed, and after one sitting under the tongue of Reverend Evans, he swore he'd never go back.

"But it wasn't just the preaching that put Grandpa off–it was that the reverend didn't take Grandpa serious. When he came to the house for dinner, the two of them got into a discussion about souls, and Grandpa brought up the spirit-stealers his father and grandfather had cautioned him about. Reverend Evans said it was superstitious nonsense, and belittled Grandpa in front of Grandma and me.

"As the reverend was leaving, Grandpa said, 'Then why don't you have a go at converting that old woman down the road?'

"To which Reverend Evans snorted back, 'I may just do that, Brother Hardy.'

"Well, two days later, on a Tuesday morning in July, I was walking to town past the old woman's place. She was standing out on the back of her property, near the bow in the river, her regular black outfit on, bent over in her garden. I could make out the old scarecrow with its broad-brimmed straw hat, flannel shirt, and black pants. The sun was ricocheting off the pie tins on the scarecrow's wrists.

"As I passed by, who comes walking up the road from town but Reverend Evans in his minister's suit and hat. We talked for a minute beside the road and he said he was going to see the old woman. I advised him I'd seen her in her garden, then pressed on for town.

"By the time I finished my business and left town for home, it was late afternoon. Still plenty of sunlight, but I knew I'd have to hustle to get back by supper.

"As I approached the old woman's place, I noticed she was still out there, bent over, weeding. At first I thought nothing of it. But a creepy feeling came over me, like a cold breeze on the back of my neck. I looked behind me, but there was nothing there. No breeze, no one watching. Something was wrong.

"I turned to look toward the woman. Gone. I wondered if she'd collapsed in the garden. I squinted, but I still couldn't make her out. So I played Good Samaritan and walked fast toward the stone wall. Then I broke into a run, scared I'd find her dead and scared to death I'd find her alive.

"I stopped at the wall. She had to be inside. There was no gate. Something–*a feeling*–stopped me from climbing over the wall. Instead I looked over the top.

"It wasn't just a garden. Mixed with the snap-peas and knee-high corn were stones, markers with faded writing on them. *It was a bone yard,* a burying ground. *The old woman was tending a grave garden.* The cold chill pricked my neck again.

"A movement to the right–I sensed as much as saw it–something black and fast ducking behind the corn. Then a rustling, but not the wind. Water. Rippling over the rocks. The river. The sound brought me back to myself.

"Something else moved, and I glanced sideways at the scarecrow. One of the pie tins held a reflection–a head, the head of the old woman, in the hood. Only it wasn't *her* face framed by the hood–it was *Reverend Evans,* eyes wide with terror, mouth flung open in a mute *scream–warning me,* warning me not to turn around. She had to be behind me, and if I turned to look, she'd have me.

"Someone's–some *thing's*–cold, damp breath on the back of my neck made me wince, and I felt an icy bite on one of the big tendons holding my head to my shoulders. I remembered what Grandpa had said.

"I sighted in on the water, shut my eyes tight and ran for the river, screaming, leaping, swatting my neck like hornets were on me, all the while praying out loud between screams, 'Now I lay me down to sleep; now I lay me down to sleep ...'

"And with who-knows-what riding my shoulders, gnawing my neck, I plunged in darkness through the reeds at the top of the bank, landing on the gravel and rocks. Scratched and cut, I clawed my way through the shallows to deep water. I stayed under longer than I ever have, letting the current carry me downstream. When I came up for air, I kept my eyes clamped shut, then went under again. I don't know how many times I did that, floating and feeling my way the two miles to town. When I climbed onto shore by the town bridge, whatever'd been on my back was gone.

"From that day on, I never again took the Back River Road. I always went the long way around.

"Everyone assumed Reverend Evans left town before the church could fire him. I never said any different. I was too afraid she'd come after me."

Todd sat rigid in his chair. Behind him, just outside the store's door, barely at the edge of his vision, something moved–something black and shadowy. It stepped into the doorway, darkening it.

A look of terror came over the three old men.

"Close your eyes!" the storyteller yelled, and Todd saw the three old men do so immediately.

Todd shut his eyes and drew his feet up from the floor, folding his arms across his chest defensively.

He heard groans and cries and scraping chairs, but he didn't look. He put his hands over his ears, but he couldn't mute what was going on around him.

"Aaaahhh! My eyes!" one of the old men yelled.

"Aaiieeyy! It's got me!" another cried. The latter cry seemed to come from someone being dragged across the floor.

Suddenly it was quiet.

Todd didn't move. He just sat, knees up, eyes shut, back stiff, hands over ears, softly chanting "Now I lay me down to sleep ..."

Finally, slowly, he opened his eyes.

No one there. Rockers empty, one still moving, another on its side on the floor.

Todd stood on shaky legs and tottered toward the open door and the warm sunlight.

"Boo!" yelled an old woman in a black scarf and shawl. Todd leaped straight up, heart stopping dead for a minute. He knew it was the witchy woman.

"They warned you!" she snarled.

Todd's eyes went wide.

"Your eyes are open!" she cackled. Todd froze as she reached for him.

"Gotcha!" a choir of voices yelled, as if this was a surprise birthday party. In a flash the three old men, the storekeeper, and the old woman (the storekeeper's wife), were there, grinning and laughing.

The five of them sat around the store with Todd for an hour, recounting this and that part of the story, recalling his expressions. The elaborate ruse had all been in fun (though it took Todd awhile to appreciate the humor).

But even today, when Todd visits the farm in the summer, whenever he walks the Injun Path near the old woman's house, he picks up his pace. He won't look toward the scarecrow. In fact, he keeps one eye–the one on that side of the road–shut tight. Because you never know, you just never know.

Woo-Woo

Sally lay on the rainbow beach towel, propped on her elbows like a human chaise lounge. The sun shone bright and hot, and the beach was wall-to-wall with people. Her best friend Carla lay like a corpse on Minnie Mouse beside her, eyes closed, tanned body absorbing the warm rays. Despite the crowd and Carla's company, Sally felt alone on the beach, isolated, as if a view from the sky would show everything and everyone in black and white, but her in color, like the soda commercials she'd seen. Except that it would have been reversed, and everyone else would be in color while she was dull and drab, black and white.

Barely twenty yards in front of her, where she could keep a close watch on him, her son Colin played at the water's edge, sand bucket and toy shovel beside him, his four-year-old body bent at the waist as he pushed his pink plastic tugboat around in inches-deep water. Two other pre-schoolers, one a blonde boy, the other a red-haired, fair-skinned girl, played beside him. Whenever someone walked across Sally's line of sight, cutting her off for a second from Colin, she'd feel her heart skip and panic begin to rise in her throat. She knew in her head there were plenty of people around, other mothers and fathers, and that someone nearby would pick him up if he fell face down in the water.

There was no danger, not really. A person had to walk fifty yards offshore before the water got to two feet deep.

But something in her chest tightened, and she could feel her face twisting and knotting each time Colin disappeared from sight for a second. She knew she was over-reacting, that this fear of losing had to do, as the counselor had pointed out, with Butch's death two winters before.

She could still picture his trawler, upside-down in the icy harbor, a quarter mile from the safety of his boat's dock, nothing but blackish-green hull above water, like a whale blowing, the thick-iced rigging that had caused the boat to capsize reaching bottomward toward the mud like a tap root. She could imagine Butch's and Chet's bodies sealed in the cabin, chilly, gasping, then still, motionless. Five of Butch's crew had escaped, swum to shore. But eight hours later, news helicopters still clove the air above the overturned vessel, their whirling rotors rippling the water's surface as divers worked to free Butch's and his best friend Chet's bodies.

Sally shivered, despite the warm sun, and checked to see that Colin was safe. He was on his hands and knees, pushing his pink tugboat in the water the way he pushed his toy dump truck in the sandbox at home. His mouth hooted a woo-woo sound for the tug whistle.

A murmur arose from the beach crowd to her left, and Sally turned to see a young man, handsome with chiseled jaw line and dark good looks, stroll past in a black tuxedo and top hat. He looked as if he might be going to a prom or a wedding. The only thing the outfit lacked was socks and shoes. He was barefoot. One hand swung by his side as he walked along the wet/dry line where the gentle, lapping waves reached. The area made a natural promenade between sunbathers and waders.

Sally's fingers touched Carla's wrist.

"Carla. Ya gotta see this."

Carla sat up and looked where Sally pointed.

The young man held a clutch of roses, perhaps a dozen, long-stemmed. When he crossed the invisible line between Sally and Colin, she leaned to the side and quick-checked that her son was all right. Colin, too, had paused to look up at the tuxedoed young man. Sally guessed him to be mid-twenties.

He continued the hundred yards to the west until he reached the town breakwater, a long, Army-Corps-of-Engineers-built rock ridge with a beacon at its end. To the east of the breakwater stretched the shallow-water bathing beach, to the west the deep-water entrance to the protected harbor. The young man made his way out onto the boulder breakwater with the agility of a mountain goat.

Sally watched him for a moment, then quickly glanced back to Colin, who was pushing his tugboat. She couldn't hear him but she could see his mouth making the woo-woo sounds and the engine noises Butch had taught him when Colin was barely two. She could see Butch in the boy, the same soft brown eyes and small-lobed ears.

Sally leaned back again, then stared at her toes, sighting down her body at them through the V between her breasts. Her toenails were plain now, unpolished. She imagined them bright red for a moment, the color Butch had once painted them when they were first married, before Colin. She could picture even now the details of that night–two wine glasses on the coffee table, an open bottle of Chardonnay, the vase of roses he'd brought home to her for no special occasion, the bayberry-scented candles they'd left burning all night and which were down to nubs in morning. And the music, James Taylor and then Van Morrison and a tape of piano music with sea sounds in the background, to which they'd made love. Even now, two years after the capsizing, though she knew he was dead and had said the word dead aloud with the counselor, she half-expected Butch to walk through the kitchen door, smile and kiss her hello, and ask as always, "What's for supper, hon?"

"Remember how handsome Butch and John and Chet looked in their tuxedoes at your wedding?" The question jolted Sally. It was Carla's voice from beside her.

"What?" Sally asked, confused. She felt like someone being roused from a sound sleep.

"That kid in the tuxedo out there." Carla pointed in the direction of the breakwater. "He reminds me of Butch and the guys in the wedding party when you guys got married. They all looked so handsome, didn't they?"

Sally looked skyward, away from Carla. She caught a deep breath as she turned her head. Her lips quivered.

"Sorry, Sal," Carla said, reaching out her hand to grip Sally's.

"It's okay," Sally said, not meaning it. She realized now that part of her had been hoping–no, actually believed for a moment–that the young man in the tuxedo would stop at her feet, stand above her unpainted toenails, and announce, "Special delivery. Roses for

Sally. With love, Butch."

Sally eye-checked Colin, who had moved a few feet to one side, then glanced at the breakwater. The young man in the tuxedo had reached the end and stood leaning against the beacon as a mountain climber might lean into a flag he has just planted at the summit.

Beyond the breakwater, a mile off, the sands of an outlying island shimmered in the heat-haze. Two sailboats passed behind the young man in the dreamy, slow-moving neverland between him and the far-off island. With sails puffed out like feathered breasts, the boats reminded Sally of a pair of swans she and Butch had fed in the oily water beside the fish dock. Butch had said swans mated for life, and once one died, the other remained single forever. At the time, it sounded romantic, a parable of devotion.

Further west, beyond the shore end of the breakwater, Sally saw a two-masted coastal schooner coming out the channel. It was either the Marietta or the Katrina, the two tall ships homeported in town. Its sails were nearly full-rigged now, and soon it would pass the end of the breakwater and be in open waters. The eyes of the crowd turned toward it as its sails billowed. Despite all its rigging and sails above its decks, the schooner barely tipped to port.

The young man in the tuxedo faced the tall ship like a patriot at a parade. Instead of placing his hand over his heart, though, he clutched the bouquet of roses to his bosom.

It's so romantic, Sally thought. *A warm sunny day. The water and the breakwater. Smaller sailboats and an island in the distance. A tall ship passing a handsome young lover in a tuxedo. Roses.* Sally's heart ached.

The schooner passed the breakwater and headed east. The young man began to wave. He held up the roses, continued waving.

A young woman near the bowsprit began to wave back. His girlfriend? Lover? Fiancee? Wife?

The young man doffed his top hat and leaned forward in a swooping bow, drawing the hat under his torso so that it almost touched the rocky breakwater. He set the hat aside and drew the long-stemmed roses from the bouquet one at a time, tossing them onto the water in a slow, dramatic fashion, the way one might pull petals off a flower and count she-loves-me, she-loves-me-not. When only the last rose remained, he clutched it to his heart the way a crying clown might, his hand making a pitter-pat motion. He slipped the last rose into the lapel of his tuxedo jacket, donned the top hat once more, and turned to begin the lonely walk home along the breakwater.

The beach crowd suddenly stood, everyone clapping and cheering, as if together they had sat through a great Broadway show.

Except Sally. To her, the crowd on its feet was like a forest that had sprung up by black magic. To her it brought panic, terror, for Colin was gone. A cry lodged in her throat as she leaped to her feet, pressing her hands into the crowd as if sorting her way through a field of reeds or parting oriental bead curtains, pushing people out of the way, sobbing and mixing up excuse-me's, look-out-move's, and my-son-my-son's.

The crowd was still clapping when she reached the water line where she'd last seen Colin playing. A half-dozen children were standing there clapping, facing not the breakwater but the crowded beach, believing the applause was for them. They all looked like Colin now, and Sally's mind scrambled to recall which bathing suit he'd been wearing. The blue one or the brown one? She found herself checking ear lobes, hoping to spot the small ones Colin had inherited from Butch.

She saw the pink tugboat in the water now, capsized, its plastic hull bobbing in the gentle waves. She sobbed, then felt the building-up scream break free of her mouth, calling the names "Colin. Butch. Colin. Colin. Colin."

"Mommy?" Her son's voice was soft, and the tiny hands which came with it tugged on the hip of her bathing suit.

She looked down and could barely make her son out through the hot, salty tears. Her shoulders sagged with relief and she squatted in the sand and inches-deep water, drawing her son to her bosom the way the young man had drawn the roses close. Her chest heaved heavy sobs and the words alternately spurted and tumbled out of her mouth.

"I couldn't see you, honey. You disappeared. I was so worried. I thought I'd lost you. You'll be all right. I'll be all right. I'll be all right."

The crowd continued its clapping, whistling, hooting. The young man was crossing the beach now on his way back to his car. A standing ovation.

"What, Mommy?" Colin asked, breaking free of her hug and leaning back to look in her eyes. "I can't hear you, Mommy."

Sally placed her hands behind the small of her son's back as if enclosing him in a hula hoop. She took a breath and said, "I said I couldn't see you, honey. Are you okay?"

Colin nodded.

"Me, too, honey," she said. "I'm okay, too."

Sally picked up the pink tugboat, emptied the water from its hollow hull, and set it right-side-up in the water.

"Is this Daddy's boat?" she asked.

"No," Colin said, his voice both matter-of-fact and annoyed. "Not *Daddy's* boat. *My* boat."

Sally bit her lip for a moment as the words sank in. Then she let her mouth relax.

"You're right, honey," she said. "You're right. That's not Daddy's boat. It's your boat."

Colin smiled. "Woo-woo," he hooted, pushing the tug along in the water.

"Woo-woo," Sally answered weakly, placing her hand over her son's and helping him push the boat. Colin laughed with glee, and her voice grew stronger. "Woo-woo," she said again, louder, more like a tugboat's whistle. "Woo-woo. Woo-woo. Woo."

Thumb Island Elephants

My name is Elvira Whipple, and I've lived here on the Thumb my whole life. I'm 94 and not real healthy, so I thought I'd tell why the Congregational Church manger scene has two elephants.

Christmas Eve 1909 I was a week shy of turning ten. It had snowed all day, so we had a foot of new snow atop a foot of old. My father was a deacon at Thumb Island Congregational Church; my mother sang in the choir. I was so eager to get to the 8 o'clock service of hymns and candles, I could hardly eat supper.

As most folks know, Thumb Island isn't an island at all. It's a village on a peninsula, with water on three sides–east, south, and west–that juts into Fisher's Island Sound like a swelled thumb. The east-west coastal railway crosses it at the north end, making it appear on a map as if the thumb's been cut off and stitched back on. As far back as I can remember, locals have simply called it the Thumb.

Back then we had five churches in the Thumb: Congregational, Baptist, Episcopal, Roman Catholic, and Shiloh. I never really understood the differences, and I can see now that much of what I learned was incorrect. What I thought my parents and other adults were saying was this.

The Episcopalians were kissing cousins to the Church of England. You didn't have to be wealthy to belong, but it helped, and it helped if you could trace your lineage. My father said they made too much of a show of their religion when they worshiped. (I later learned that they were very *liturgical.)*

The Baptists were similar to us Congregationalists except they dunked people to baptize them. We sprinkled ours. Baptist prayers were longer, too.

The Catholics were people we were supposed to avoid. Many were from Europe–fishermen and their families who didn't speak much English. They made the sign of the cross when they passed their own church. Episcopalians, Congregationalists, and Baptists, on the other hand, made a point of crossing the street to avoid meeting the Catholic priest. For reasons I did not understand, Catholicism was the farthest thing from Protestantism. Still, we bought fish from the Catholics, and to me it tasted the same as Protestant-caught fish.

I don't know if Shiloh was a black Baptist or a black Methodist church or something else. But it was down near the railroad tracks. Its members were mostly the families of railroad porters or ships' stewards. Some folks called it Shiloh Church, but most said "the colored church." I had no idea what Shilohs believed, but I loved to go by their church in summer when the doors windows were open, so I could hear them sing.

If there was anything like an Ecumenical Movement back in 1909, it never got across the tracks and into the Thumb.

I thought we'd never leave for church that night, but finally we did. We walked through the deep snow and arrived out of breath. My mother went to the balcony to join the choir, and my father walked to the pulpit to talk with the minister about communion.

The organ prelude filled the church. I sat back and inhaled the smells of the church as if they were my lifeblood–the slight mustiness, the polished pews, the candles, the heat from the downstairs wood furnace rising up through the floor registers. When I opened my eyes and looked behind me at the clock hung from the back balcony, it said one minute before eight. The organ prelude ended and the congregation hushed for the opening anthem.

A loud voice shattered the silence.

"Friends! We need your help."

I spun around and looked back toward the doors that led from the foyer into the sanctuary. Directly under the clock stood a black man in a suit, his hands stretched in front of him as if he were preparing to direct the choir. I recognized him as one of the porters.

No one moved.

"A wagon's stuck on the tracks. We can't get it off."

We all stared at him. This was the first time any black person had ever set foot in our church.

"Please," he pleaded. "It's a big circus wagon."

The church emptied, everyone following him to the grade crossing. There were no passenger trains on Christmas Eve, but there might be a freight. Most nights we could count on one around 11:30.

At the crossing we found a huge wagon, like one I'd seen for transporting prisoners, over on its side. This one, though, was bright red with gold trim. It was longer than two stagecoaches and built like a small railroad boxcar, and across its ends it said Barnum &

Bailey, the Greatest Show on Earth. The wagon had small slits for windows on either end. A man stood at one of the windows, talking into it, cooing softly the way you'd calm a baby. A team of four brown and white draft horses stood there, still hitched.

Four or five black men stood holding lanterns. The Shiloh crowd must have arrived first, since their church was only a hundred yards from the crossing.

After a minute or two, two small crowds arrived, Episcopalians and Baptists, led by a different black man from Shiloh. Right behind the black man was the Baptist minister in his white shirt, black suit, and overcoat. He was followed by the Episcopal rector with his black robe still on and showing from under his coat.

I could tell from the way the snow was tramped down around the wagon and from the sweat on their faces, that the Shiloh people had been struggling awhile with the wagon.

"What happened?' my father asked, and the man who had been cooing into the wagon stepped toward him.

"I was driving this team from Providence to New York for Barnum and Bailey. I stayed in Westerly last night, then got back on the road west. The storm caught me this morning and I don't think I made six miles. The horses were worn out, so I headed for Thumb Island. I hit the tracks a little off square and when the wagon tilted, the elephants must've shifted their weight inside so the wagon tipped."

"Elephants?" my father said.

"Yeah, a mother and a little one. Barnum and Bailey bought them from a Providence zoo."

I sneaked over by the wagon's slitted window. A

black girl named Hannah, about my age, stood beside me with a lantern. We peered in.

I had never seen an elephant before, only pictures. The mother lay on her side, and the flank which showed looked dusty. It rose and fell like a swelling sea. Her head was massive, and under it I could see a crumpled ear as big as my coat if I spread it on the ground.

"Look at that eye," Hannah said. "It's beautiful like a cow eye." It was true. The huge eye had the same foolish, gentle look as a cow staring over a fence, waiting for a handful of grass.

The baby stood by the mother, not nursing, just standing. They stared up at us, and the mother sort of sighed. I expected the smell of manure to drift out the barred window, but what I breathed in was more the scent of a baby after a bath, a fresh-bread smell. I wanted to touch them, to learn what their hide felt like, to see if it felt like my teacher said it would, not rough and dry, but soft and silky.

"Hey, look," someone said, and Hannah and I stepped back. There came the Catholics, their new, handsome, young, black-haired priest in his robes, leading the procession.

"What's wrong?" he asked.

"Two elephants in the wagon," my father said.

"And we can't get them out?" he said.

"The doors are on either side of the wagon," the driver said. "Which means one is against the track and the other is aiming straight up."

"Can we tip it back up?" the priest asked.

The wagon driver shook his head. "No. It's not just the weight of the wagon. You've got a five ton elephant plus the baby. Every time we try to right it, they get nervous and shift their weight, forcing us back down."

"How about getting them out first, then moving it?" our church's minister said.

The Episcopal rector thought that was a good idea, and suggested chopping a hole and removing one entire end of the wagon. But the wagon driver reminded us the wagon had been reinforced with iron bars.

"Remember," he said. "It's designed to hold an elephant."

The mother elephant trumpeted, and we all jumped back.

"Excuse me," said the black man who had burst into our church. "The land is flat here at the grade crossing, so we're always trying to lift the wagon up. What if we skid the wagon along on top of the tracks—like hauling a boat? It's only two hundred yards to the cove beach, where the track runs on top of that rock pile. The beach is lower, and we can tip the wagon down. Be a lot easier."

Everyone stared at the man, then looked to the wagon driver who shrugged his shoulders.

"Worth a try," the driver said. "But we'll need a wider path than a train. See?" He pointed out that there was a foot of new snow on the track and two feet alongside.

"We'll have to clear it," the priest said flatly. He made a megaphone with his hands and announced, first in English, then in a language that might have been Portuguese or Italian, "Friends, we must clear a wide path to the beach so we can drag the wagon there. Hurry."

In no time we had a hundred or more people, all carrying shovels, ropes, and chains. Two oxen appeared and some horses. By 10:15 we had a wide path cleared to the cove. The oxen and horses were hooked up, folks tied on more ropes, and every person there grabbed on like it was a tug-of-war at the County Fair. And we all pulled. My Lord, did we pull.

The wagon came by inches and feet, slow because we had to keep changing positions. Hannah and I pulled at the start, until my father gave us each a lantern and told us to stand on the rock trestle in case we had to signal an approaching freight train. Two other girls took lanterns down the track to the east and stood watch there.

A tiny breeze stung me and Hannah as we stood exposed on the rock trestle, and our teeth chattered. While we shivered, everyone else heaved and sweated. We could see them wiping their foreheads with their sleeves.

After we'd been out there awhile, Hannah asked me, "Elvira, you think we'll beat the train?"

I said, "God only knows," which felt true.

We looked down the railway bed toward the wagon. The piled-up snow on either side of the track made it look like a tunnel with no roof. Dozens and dozens of lanterns sat on the banked white snow, like luminaria, lighting the way, lovelier than any Christmas candle-light service I've seen since.

Down along the track, groaning and sweating, inching that wagon toward us to save those lovely, lovely elephants, we could see black folks and white folks, horses and oxen, Catholics and Protestants, the dunked and the sprinkled, working side by side. Lordy, I thought, what God wouldn't give to have me and Hannah's view. Then as soon as I thought it, I realized

God was right there with us, an arm around each of us.

A little after 11:30 we finally got the wagon positioned on the track above the beach. We set the horses and oxen up on the south side of the track. Anyone not handling animals went to the north. The people were to pull it so it started sliding downhill while the animals were to be counterweights slowing the slide.

The plan worked perfectly. Almost. We pulled, and the wagon shifted balance. Then Zoot! It slid, yanking the horses and oxen ten feet backward. Ka-whump! It hit the frozen beach. All four wheels snapped like soda crackers.

But the wagon stayed upright.

The elephants trumpeted and banged against the inner walls, terrified. Then they were silent and we all hushed. I looked down and Hannah was clutching my hand.

"Lord, bless these elephants," she whispered.

"Amen," I said.

The wagon driver held up a lantern and peered in. "They're okay," he said.

We all cheered. People began shaking hands and hugging, forgetting they were white and black, Catholic and Protestant. You'd have thought a hometown boy had just won a big race. Some people sat in the snow and wept. I don't know if the tears had to do with the elephants, or the exhaustion, or seeing folks together like that.

Then somebody yelled, "It's Christmas Day!" It was my father, holding up his pocket watch up and pointing to it. I never saw him so excited.

Someone started in with O Come, All Ye Faithful, and before long everyone was singing together. That's what we were doing five minutes later when the freight roared through–singing and smiling. The engineer must have seen the tunnel of lights and thought it was a Christmas celebration for him. He cut his speed in half, waved from the locomotive's cab and grinned, yelling Merry Christmas as if he were Santa passing by in his sleigh.

The wagon driver moved the elephants to a horse shed behind Shiloh Church, and all Christmas Day people came to visit them. It looked strange, seeing folks from all around lined up at the Shiloh Church to see the Thumb Island Christmas Elephants, which is what we called them.

The day after that a replacement wagon showed up and took the mother and baby on the rest of their journey.

That's why the Congregational Church's manger scene has two gray papier-mache elephants that are about 85 years old. I made the dark-skinned one and my lifelong best friend Hannah made the light-skinned one.

Or maybe it was the other way around.

Doesn't matter.

Whinny

Lordy, didn't my sister Whinny love horses. Momma always said horses would be the death of her.

When Whinny was a little girl, she had white porcelain horses on her bedroom bureau, watercolors and drawings and paint-by-numbers mustangs on her walls, books and magazines about thoroughbreds and quarter horses and cow ponies stacked under her bed and on her book shelf. In her desk drawer she had maps and detailed plans for a trip to Assateague and Chincoteague Islands, where she yearned to go to visit Misty and the other wild ponies she'd seen in a travelogue that once preceded a Saturday double feature at the movies. She loved the movies *Gallant Bess, National Velvet,* and a Disney flick called *Tonka. Tonka* seemed to be the turning point for her, because she stopped talking about horse racing then and got into Native American spirituality.

Some time around age nine she started signing her name Whinny instead of Winnie, arguing, "Who's to say the nickname for Winifred (her given name) isn't spelled like the horse sound?" She never went back to the old spelling after that. She was always Whinny, while I suffered under the names Robbie, Bobby, Rob, Bob, Roberto and Robert–except with Whinny. She mostly called me Boob.

Whinny remained constant, always sure of herself and what she loved. She was crazy about horses and devoted her life to learning about them and living with them.

She never took horseback riding lessons. Mom said we couldn't afford it. But in truth it was because Whinny never asked to take lessons. She never climbed on a horse's back, for she thought it was cruel and demeaning to the noble horse. She wouldn't even get on a merry-go-round when the carnival came to town, nor would she let a fireman lead her around a roped ring on a pony at the Fire Department Block Party. She loved petting the ponies' manes and flanks, and she'd talk to them for hours at a time the way a mother coos and sings to her baby.

She reveled in the smell of manure, and I once saw her run into a parade with a dustpan to scoop up a fresh horse turd that was dropped by the grand marshall's steed. She took it home and let it stink up her room for three days before Mom made her put it outside.

When Whinny turned twelve, she blew out the candles on her cake, which was in the shape of a horse, of course, and announced that she was going to live on a farm in Vermont when she grew up. No husband. No kids. Just her and horses. Maybe some chickens. Her announcement caused hardly a ripple. Neither my father, my mother, nor I was surprised. And from that day on, my sister Whinny, of single-minded purpose, organized her life around that dream

I don't know how she discovered it, but she found as was accepted at Sterling, a tiny alternative college in Craftsbury, Vermont, an hour north of Montpelier. She was impressed by the fact that students could take a class in which they learned to plow a field using oxen, or another class in sheep shearing. It was a place where a student could learn to properly skin and cook a rabbit, something the valedictorian demonstrated in lieu of giving a speech the year Whinny graduated.

My sister was salutatorian in that graduating class of five seniors, and gave a speech about the spirituality of horses. She closed the remarks by reading a moving poem about a man and his bond with his two plow horses, Blackie and Bill, around the time of the advent of wheeled tractors. Mom and Dad clapped, but I found myself weak and moved to tears at my sister Whinny's horse theology.

"Robbie," she said afterward, while I was trying to find words to tell her how proud I was of her, "that's Griff, the professor who taught me horseshoeing."

I swallowed the lump in my throat and looked in the direction she was pointing, dropping what I'd been attempting to do.

For five years after graduation, Whinny lived on a Vermont hill farm outside Derby Line, near the Canadian border. It wasn't her farm, it belonged to the Parkers, an older couple who lived most of the year in Florida and spent their summers and early fall in New England.

Whinny was the farm's caretaker, keeping the house, barn, and outbuildings heated and repaired. She improved her chainsaw skills and worked with the Parkers' four horses sledding logs in from the woods to where she could cut and split them for firewood. She had six goats and milked two of them. She wrote a column for two years, *This Solitary Life,* for the local newspaper, then self-syndicated it to a dozen other weekly

Vermont papers. She published a piece on maple sugaring in *Vermont Life* magazine, and the picture of her and her horses hauling sap made the cover. Mom and Dad and I all got framed copies of that cover photo. Whinny and her horses.

The first year after her graduation from Sterling, midway between Thanksgiving and Christmas, I went to visit Whinny in Derby Line. She'd been caretaking six months by then. The second afternoon she talked me into going snowshoeing.

"Aw, come on, Boob," she needled. Most people were calling me Rob by then, except for my fraternity brothers who called me Bobo.

It was exhausting, snowshoeing, but Whinny fluffed along on the soft show as if she'd been born and raised in the Klondike. I finally caught up with her near a stone wall that overlooked an open meadow.

"This is where I want to be buried," she said, pulling her knitted cap from her head. Seeing my surprise, she quickly amended, "Some day, that is."

She talked about the beauty of the spot and pointed out a half dozen graves that dated back to the 1870's and 1880's. The stone wall we were leaning against was only one of four walls that enclosed an old cemetery.

"Just think," she said. "These people never saw an automobile. They were horse people." Her eyes were stone serious, not exactly envious, but reverent. Then she broke the spell by pointing to something above my head.

I looked up. Nailed to a board above what had been the entrance gate was a horseshoe.

"Tips facing up," Whinny said with a smile, making the same U-shape with her thumb and fingers. "To hold the good luck."

I made a scrunchy face and asked, "Is it still a real cemetery?"

"Sure it's a real cemetery. See the graves? It's part of the Parkers' farm. They said they'd like to be buried here, too. Just think," she said, "no one's lain down here in a hundred years."

There was something poetic–no, breathtaking–about the way Whinny said it. Not "no one's *been laid down*", but "no one's *lain down* here in a hundred years." What a feel my sister had for language and drama and beauty. I sensed it came from being so focused, so single-minded, from loving horses.

Before we left the cemetery, Whinny recited Robert Frost's *Stopping By Woods on a Snowy Evening* from memory. After that visit, I went home and memorized it myself.

Last year Whinny died in a stable fire at a county fair. It was late at night, just after the fairgrounds emptied out. Suddenly there were flames. Whinny and another woman ran in and threw open the gates to free the horses. But the animals were terrified and bolted, knocking Whinny down in their panic. A hoof must have struck her in the head. The other woman got out. Eight horses died in the fire.

When Mom, Dad, and I got the news, we were devastated. For the first day or two I wanted to blame the horses, because they had made Whinny care so much that she jeopardized her own safety. Then I wanted to blame Whinny, again for caring too much and thereby causing her own death. But I stopped that when Whinny came to me in a dream and said, "Oh Boob, Boob, Boob. It wasn't the horses' fault."

We held a graveside service in the little cemetery on the Parker farm, burying Whinny as close as we could to the gate with the lucky horseshoe.

I had planned to recite the Frost poem, but a wave of grief overcame me and my memory failed. I started off: *Whose woods these are, I think I know.*

That's all I could remember. The others all closed their eyes as if it was a prayer.

Finally I heard Mrs. Parker's soft voice break the silence: *And miles to go before I sleep, miles to go before I sleep.*

Whinny's words came back to me–*No one's lain down here in a hundred years*–and it occurred to me she'd have liked this. She'd have liked this, lying down with horse people.

Lordy, didn't my sister Whinny love horses.

O R D E R F O R M

Burt Creations

PLEASE SEND ME THE FOLLOWING:

QUAN.	ITEM	PRICE
_____	Odd Lot Paperback Book ($14.95)	_______
_____	A Christmas Dozen Paperback Book ($14.95)	_______
_____	A Christmas Dozen Double cassette ($15.95)	_______
_____	A Christmas Dozen Double CD ($16.95)	_______
_____	Unk's Fiddle Hardcover Book ($15.95)	_______
_____	Unk's Fiddle Paperback ($13.95)	_______
	SHIPPING	_______
	SALES TAX	_______
	TOTAL	_______

Priority Mail Shipping & handling is $4.50 first item, $2.50 per additional item. Connecticut residents add 6% sales tax.

FREE SHIPPING ON ORDERS OF MORE THAN 10 UNITS

NAME ______________________________

ADDRESS ______________________________

CITY __________ STATE __________ ZIP __________

TELEPHONE __________ FAX __________ EMAIL __________

PAYMENT:

❑ Checks payable to: Burt Creations
Mail to: 29 Arnold Place, Norwich, CT 06360

❑ VISA ❑ MasterCard

Cardnumber:______________________________
Name on card:______________________________
Exp. Date: ________(mo) ________(year)

- Toll free order phone 1-866-MyDozen (866-693-6936 / Secure message machine) Give mailing/shipping address, telephone number, MC/Visa name & card number plus expiration date.
- Secure Fax orders: 860-889-4068. Fill out this form & fax.
- On-line orders: www.burtcreations.com
  order@burtcreations.com

http://www.burtcreations.com